What Color Is God?

Cynthia A. Wragg

ISBN 978-1-64140-220-0 (paperback)
ISBN 978-1-64258-588-9 (hardcover)
ISBN 978-1-64140-221-7 (digital)

Christian Faith Publishing, Inc.
832 Park Avenue
Meadville, PA 16335
www.christianfaithpublishing.com

Printed in the United States of America

For my girls
Courtney and Alexis

"I will praise thee forever, because thou hast done it…" PS. 52:9

One afternoon Cookie and Lexi sat on the porch sky watching. They often spent hours together, laughing, playing, and watching television. Today they were studying the sky. They loved gazing at the clear blue sky dotted with fluffy white clouds that floated like balls of cotton candy. The sun was beaming so brightly that day that they had to shield their eyes just to look up.

Cookie was Lexi's older cousin. She taught Lexi her ABCs, numbers, and colors. She showed her how to tie her shoes. But Cookie's favorite thing was reading Bible stories to Lexi. She read stories about Noah, Moses, and Baby Jesus. She taught Lexi that God loved the people of the world so much that He let His Son Jesus die so man could live.

As the afternoon passed, the sky changed from bright blue to a dull gray. The blazing sun disappeared behind a huge dark rain cloud. Pretty soon big raindrops were dancing on the sidewalk in front of the porch. Cookie and Lexi went inside.

"Cookie," said Lexi, "read me a story. Read about Joseph and his coat of many colors."

Cookie pulled out her Bible storybook and read to Lexi all about Joseph and his brothers.

At the end of the story, Lexi clapped her hands and squealed joyfully, "Yay-y-y-y! I love that story!"

Cookie closed the book, and there on the cover was a picture of Joseph and his beautiful coat of many colors. Lexi gently ran her fingers across the picture and smiled to herself as if she knew something that no one else knew.

All of a sudden she looked wide-eyed at Cookie and asked wonderingly, "Cookie, what color is God?"

Up till now Cookie had never really thought of God as being any special color. He was God. He did not need to be a color. But because Lexi asked, Cookie wanted to give her a really good answer that she could understand.

So in her heart Cookie whispered a quick prayer to God.

"Dear God, please help me explain to Lexi what color you are. Thank you. Amen."

Cookie listened quietly for God's reply, and after only a few moments, she heard the answer to her prayer. Cookie took Lexi's hands and whispered, "Remember the rainbow in the story about Noah's Ark?"

Lexi replied softly, "Yes, I remember."

Then Cookie said thoughtfully, "God is like that rainbow… and Joseph's coat. He's many colors."

Lexi's eyes widened as she echoed, "Many colors?"

"That's right. He is many colors," repeated Cookie. There was silence for a minute. Then Cookie said, "You see, Lexi…

God is yellow like the big round sun that sets the sky ablaze.

And green like the slender blades of grass on which the brown cows graze.

He's red like the blood that Jesus shed way back on Calvary,

And He's white 'cause that's the color that stands for purity.

And like the great big sky above, our God is a lovely blue.

Then at night when the sun has disappeared, he becomes a darker hue.

God's orange, purple, pink, and bronze. He's gold and silver too.

He's even a beautiful shade of brown, just like me and you!

So you see God is many colors, and through our eyes we see

The exact shade of whatever color we want God to be."

Lexi carefully thought this over. All the lovely colors of the rainbow and of Joseph's coat flashed through her mind. She imagined seeing the face of God in all those colors. Then she flashed a huge toothy grin and said, "You know what, Cookie?"

"What?" asked Cookie.

"God sure is pretty, just like the rainbow," Lexi said, smiling.

Cookie and Lexi moved to the window and looked out. The rain had slowed to a drizzle, then stopped. The sun popped out from behind a thick silver cloud, and its rays reached down to the earth like long slender fingers.

All of a sudden Cookie shouted, "Look, Lexi, look!"

There in the distance shone the biggest, most beautiful rainbow Cookie had ever seen. It stretched from one end of the earth to the other in a perfect arch. There were shades of green, yellow, orange, pink, and purple. It was awesome! Lexi clapped her hands and squealed in delight.

Cookie smiled and whispered in Lexi's ear, "You're right, Lexi. God is really pretty!"

About the Author

Courtesy of Wendy Rogers Photography

Cynthia A. Wragg was born and raised in Georgetown, South Carolina. After earning a bachelor's degree in communications from Winthrop College, Rock Hill, South Carolina, she returned to her hometown and began a career in radio broadcasting. Because of her love of children, she eventually entered the field of education and taught reading and language arts to special needs children at Tara Hall Home for Boys in Georgetown county. She later furthered her education by earning a master's degree in human resources development from Webster University, Myrtle Beach, South Carolina. She currently resides in Georgetown. This is her first book.

CPSIA information can be obtained
at www.ICGtesting.com
Printed in the USA
LVHW071135280620
659213LV00043B/2358

9 781642 585889